Stand Where You're Afraid

D.V. Morse

Published by D.V. Morse, 2024.

STAND WHERE YOU'RE AFRAID

First edition. March 28, 2024.

Copyright © 2024 D.V. Morse.

ISBN: 979-8224175307

Written by D.V. Morse.

Tags and Content Alerts

Genre: Modern with magic

Rating: Explicit

Trigger warnings: references to past intimate partner violence (not between main characters), pregnancy loss, abortion, an act of domestic terrorism, character turned into a paranormal creature against their will

Character Features: vampirism, lycanthropy (werewolf), f/f relationship, past f/m relationship

Other Tags: werewolf pack dynamics

Acknowledgements

First and foremost, I want to thank Chloe Parker for organizing the *I Am the Fire* anthology in which this novella first appeared. Without that fundraising project in the wake of the Dobbs decision, this would not exist. I'm sure managing all of us was very much like herding cats, and she herded us very professionally.

Thanks also to the B'write Moon critique group, who gave extremely helpful feedback while I whipped this into shape for the anthology, and to Lillian Lippold, whose editing was just what was needed to bring it to the next level.

Finally, but far from least, thanks to all of my cheerleaders, including family, friends, and Twitch chatters. You've helped me keep going when I wanted to give up.

The title is inspired by a line from the Halestorm song "I Am the Fire" after which the anthology was named. I may possibly have listened to the song on repeat while drafting this.

Front cover is by Liz Bank Design, LLC.

Chapter 1

Adrienne drained the last drops of beer from her bottle. The peaceful lights of the Thames River glimmered as she leaned over the club's deck, music pulsing in the background. She wondered if she'd ever see the original river this one was named for. England wasn't on her list of top tourist destinations, but she had all the time in the world. New London, Connecticut might be home for now, but it probably wouldn't be forever. Giving the beer bottle a shake, she turned and went back inside to get rid of it, the music growing louder as she stepped in. As restful as the river view on the deck was, she had some energy to burn off. That was best done on the dance floor.

"Ready for another, Elvira?" the skinny bartender asked with a grin that lit up his ebony face.

Being a paper-pale night shift nurse with raven black hair meant a lot of vampire jokes. Adrienne hadn't found those funny even before she'd been turned. Now that she was one, well, she was completely done with being compared to some campy actress who hadn't even played an actual vampire character.

"That wasn't funny the last fifty times, Darius," she told the bartender as she pushed her empty beer bottle across the counter. "Keep it up, and I'll rip your throat out."

"You can try," he said, chuckling.

Adrienne shook her head and walked away, an involuntary smile tugging at her lips. Vampire versus werewolf was not a guaranteed win in either direction, but she was pretty sure she could take him. Not that she planned to. It was a long-running joke between them, the moves as practiced as any dance routine. Darius was a good guy, one of the first to prove to her that getting turned didn't have to mean becoming a monster. At least he'd given her some insight into how things worked for werewolves, Even though there didn't seem to be a vampire equivalent to a pack, learning how the werewolves managed things had helped her find her way.

More importantly, the music was picking up, and that was what she'd been waiting for. The plus side to being both night shift nurse and vampire was that, when she actually got a weekend off, she could absolutely party all night. Fortunately, the bars around here all closed well before dawn. Not that she'd incinerate into a pile of dust or something if the sun's rays touched her. That'd make going home from work kind of impossible. The sun just leached her energy; all she wanted to do once it was up was go to sleep.

The shot boy came around with Jolly Ranchers, one of which she downed quickly. She replaced the test tube in the rack of his tray and refused the change he offered after her payment. He gave her a grin that looked misplaced on his otherwise grumpy face. She just shrugged and moved on. She'd done that job or the next thing to it for plenty of years to put herself through school. Making a server's day made hers a little better too.

Not everyone on the floor was a monster. She could smell at least a few humans in the mosaic of dancers. Some of them had probably wandered in by accident, not realizing Darius' club was for people like her, and they danced obliviously with werewolves, shifters, and even the occasional fae or demigod. Others were in the know, specifically present because of the clientele. One human had confided to her in the past that she just liked the thrill of dating someone "different." She'd never understood humans who did that, but to each their own. And anyway, it was impossible to tell the oblivious from the thrill-seekers, so she just ignored them all.

She just liked to dance, and the spells Darius had gotten his witch friend to cast on the place made it safe for everyone, humans, part-humans, and non-humans alike. It didn't even have bar fights, it was so safe. She made her way onto the dance floor, squeezing past a siren and a ghoul to find a spot for herself. She closed her eyes and let the music carry her, riding the bass line, veering off to the melody, and then working her way back along the drums.

Dancing used to be her way to temporarily shut her brain off. That didn't quite work anymore; she couldn't help hearing literally every non-undead person's heartbeat in counterpoint to the music. Someone here tonight had a slight arrhythmia, which tried to switch her nurse brain into gear. She firmly informed it that she was off the clock, and anyway, lots of people threw the occasional palpitation. Another heartbeat drew her attention. Strong, steady, and in sync with the music. Focusing on that, she found the rest of the noise melted away the way it used to. She let the music and that heartbeat erase everything else, until she forgot she was a vampire, and there was nothing but the rhythm.

Someone bumped into her, and she sidestepped, putting her back to them without even opening her eyes. Another thing that had changed since her human days. Back then, a move like that, which definitely felt deliberate, would've had her on high alert. Now? Even if the place weren't spelled to hell and back—literally, unless she missed her guess about why the one type of monster she never saw here was a demon—she was probably the most dangerous person in the room. There were some advantages to being a vampire, even if she didn't like to make use of them.

The same person bumped into her. This time Adrienne's eyes shot open in annoyance, and she found herself face to face with an athletic blond woman, deeply tanned despite summer being long gone. She was wearing a brown leather jacket over some band t-shirt, plain jeans, and surprisingly pink sneakers. Werewolf, by her scent and golden eyes. Pretty, but annoying. And also the owner of that heartbeat she'd been dancing to.

Interesting.

"Might want to open your eyes," the woman said.

"Might want to watch where you're going," Adrienne replied. It came out less sharply than she'd intended.

"Who says I wasn't?"

Well, that was interesting. The werewolf stepped closer just as the music slid from one song to the next and the lights went from sweeping to strobing. The energy in the club cranked up a notch along with the wolf's heartbeat, the floor shaking as the dancers joined in with the bouncier beat. Somehow, the wolf's moves still seemed fluid, even as she punctuated each beat with hips, shoulders, or both. Adrienne had no idea how she managed that, but watching her was almost enjoyable enough for Adrienne to stop dancing herself. She smiled at the thought.

She did still have a lot of restless energy, though, and this song was just the thing to spend it on.

The press of the crowd was usually something Adrienne resisted. Tonight, she rolled with it, and soon, she and the wolf were dancing well into each other's personal space. They weren't quite in sync, but she didn't care. It had been a very, very long time since anyone had caught her attention like this. The heartbeat, still in sync with the music. The mixture of fluid and sharp movements. Something about this werewolf was fascinating.

The other woman took Adrienne's hand and guided her in a tight half-turn before pulling her close. Adrienne drank in her warmth as if she'd been starved for it.

"Like this," she murmured in Adrienne's ear as she made another smooth-yet-sharp move, plastering Adrienne's back to her own front, a hand on Adrienne's hip. "Name's Marla, by the way. You are refreshingly cool."

Adrienne snorted at the pun but went with it. This was definitely better than watching.

It took a few tries before she was really able to match Marla's serpentine movements. Shoulders and chest forward, then rolling back and letting the energy of the song and the movement roll down their spines and all the way to their feet. Then everything clicked into place. Adrienne was back to riding the music. And Marla. She decided that was a damn fine combination as Marla's breasts pressed into her back on the next roll.

As the music shifted, Marla's dancing shifted from smooth and snaky to sharp snaps of shoulders and hips. Then she layered the two together, like she'd been doing earlier. Each time, Adrienne caught on faster, until they were both following the music so smoothly, Adrienne didn't have to think about it at all. This is what dancing used to be, what she kept wanting it to be again. It was almost like returning to her human self, something she could hardly remember at times.

When the next song ended and Marla whispered, "Do you want to get out of here?" all Adrienne could do was nod. If that was the next move, she'd continue to follow. She'd always had a weak spot for a woman who knew what she wanted.

⎯⎯⎯◉⎯⎯⎯

Adrienne didn't bring strange werewolves home often (or, well, ever), but her apartment was the closest and she didn't want to lose the groove they'd gotten into. As well as they moved together on the dance floor, she couldn't wait to find out how well they'd move together in bed. It took her a couple of seconds to remember how to get the basic security wards to allow Marla in, but once she had pressed the wolf's thumb against the right rune on the doorframe, they were successful. Adrienne shut the door and pushed her up against it.

"Ground rules," she said. "No teeth, especially fangs. No claws."

"Afraid I'm gonna turn you into some kind of hybrid, vampire?" Marla asked with a smirk.

"What? No. Just not into it." Adrienne shook her head to clear the decidedly unsexy image that had evoked. Sex, for her, was about trying to forget what she'd become as much as anything, and that didn't work if she or her partner shifted even partially. "Also, I kind of like my bed when it's not torn up. What about you?"

"Works for me. I'll let you know if something's not fun. Now, can we get to it?"

Adrienne let her eyes drift down along Marla's body then back up to meet her gaze, then slammed their lips together and licked her way into the heat of Marla's mouth. Marla gave as good as she got, spinning them around and pinning Adrienne against the door. It had been a long time since she'd had someone whose strength could match hers. Adrienne decided she liked it. She pushed Marla's shirt and bra up, so she could feel the breasts that had been pressed up against her earlier. She rolled a nipple between her fingers.

"Mm, your hands are so cool."

"Problem?"

"Opposite."

Adrienne grinned when Marla pulled back to rip her clothes out of the way. Adrienne took the opportunity to ditch her t-shirt and bra too.

"You gonna show me where the bedroom is, or are we gonna do this right here?" Marla growled, her eyes gleaming.

Adrienne's eyes darted briefly to her living room and almost settled on the shelf of photos before she snapped her focus back to the woman she was with. She grabbed Marla's hand and dragged her down the short hallway, very firmly not glancing into the living room as they passed. She twirled Marla as if they were dancing again and watched her tumble gracefully onto the bed. When she hit the sheets, she even struck a pose like some damn model.

"That'd be more effective without the jeans," Adrienne said. She made short work of her own jeans, sneakers, and everything else.

"You could do something about it," Marla replied with a grin.

Adrienne crawled onto the bed, rolled Marla onto her back, and kissed her again, this time burying her fingers in the silky golden hair before bracing herself with one hand as she worked Marla's jeans open with the other. After kissing her way down Marla's body, she stopped briefly to flick her tongue over Marla's nipples, teasing them harder than they already were. Marla moaned in appreciation, but was clearly impatient, pushing at Adrienne's shoulders.

Taking the hint but still savoring each taste, Adrienne worked her way lower, peppering kisses along the werewolf's belly until she reached her hips. She knelt back and yanked Marla's jeans and underwear down in one movement, shoes tugged off to rid herself of the rest of her clothes. She took in the sight of the beautifully naked woman on her usually empty bed, legs parted invitingly, before diving in.

She nuzzled Marla's curls and breathed in her musk before spreading her open and tracing her folds with her tongue. She went slowly at first, allowing her to get used to the coolness. Sometimes, this was a deal-breaker. Not tonight. At least, not yet.

She circled her tongue around Marla's clit briefly before licking her way inside, relishing her taste. Immunity to, well, everything was one of the few pluses of being a vampire, one that Adrienne really appreciated in moments like this.

Adrienne closed her eyes and focused on the silky feel of Marla's skin, the sound of her heartbeat echoing in the pulse at her core, the sheer, exuberant aliveness of her. It was more intoxicating than alcohol.

Marla moaned in either pleasure or frustration, possibly both, as Adrienne fucked her with her tongue. Taking pity on her, Adrienne thumbed Marla's clit and was rewarded with a rush of tart warmth. Marla pushed at her shoulders again though, and Adrienne pulled back to look up at her warily.

Their eyes met, and Adrienne tried to figure out why Marla had stopped her. What was wrong?

"Want to taste you too," Marla growled.

Oh. Well, that worked too. Adrienne shifted until she had her knees against Marla's shoulders. She hissed with pleasure as Marla flicked her tongue across Adrienne's clit and then pressed a deliciously warm finger inside her. It took a few moments to find just the right rhythm, but once they did, it was like they were dancing again, only so, so much better. Movement and pleasure braided and coiled around them.

As she hurtled toward her climax, Adrienne pulled her mouth off Marla, instead stroking her with the flat of her fingertips. Pleasure coursed through her and threatened to break her control over her form, her fangs struggling to reveal themselves. This was why she hardly ever did this. One of the most human things she could do, and it brought out the monster in her, or tried to.

As she attempted to hold back her change, Adrienne felt her orgasm crash over her. Marla bucked beneath her and moaned. When Adrienne bent to suckle her clit, Marla's legs clamped on either side of Adrienne's head, and Marla cried out her own pleasure. Adrienne hummed in satisfied response.

Deliciously loose-limbed, Adrienne disentangled them and stretched out next to Marla. If she closed her eyes, she could almost imagine it was five years ago, and the woman next to her was Monica. A pang of grief reminded her that wasn't fair to anyone. Not Marla, not Monica, and definitely not Adrienne, who's high was ebbing much too quickly now. Still, it was nice having a warm body in bed with her. A body she ought to be encouraging to get dressed and go home. She didn't feel like it though. That was ... weird.

Marla curled toward her, and Adrienne kissed her before pulling the tangled sheets up over them both. Marla's eyes blinked open, full of questions.

Fair enough. Adrienne hadn't realized she was going to do that either.

"Got somewhere to be?" Adrienne asked.

"No." It wasn't quite a question, but it wasn't not a question either.

"Then you might as well stick around. I might even have something that'll pass for breakfast."

Marla's eyes fell closed again, and Adrienne let herself be pulled close. Obviously, Marla was a cuddler. Adrienne was surprisingly okay with that. Her fingertips found a patch of rough skin on Marla's shoulder. Some type of scar. A question tried to form in her mind but dissipated as sleep overtook her.

Chapter 2

It was late afternoon when Adrienne stirred. There was more sun coming through the drapes than she preferred, especially considering she had the day off. Next to her, Marla grumbled and burrowed into the pillows, obviously not ready to be awake either. Werewolves weren't as nocturnal as vampires, but they weren't typically early risers either.

Breakfast. Adrienne had sort of promised breakfast. What had she been thinking?

She hauled herself out of bed and threw on a t-shirt and sweatpants. She sorted through last night's discarded clothes, threw her own into the hamper and, after a moment's hesitation, pulled her chair from the desk to drape Marla's clothes over. She considered taking a quick shower but decided that could wait.

First things first. She put on the coffee. Marla might or might not drink it, but Adrienne definitely needed a cup.

Her refrigerator wasn't exactly full of werewolf-appropriate food choices. Marla probably was big on red meat extra-raw, but not straight-up blood. It wasn't that Adrienne didn't eat regular food. She didn't *need* it, but she could eat it. She still enjoyed a good steak now and then, but when she got a hankering for it, she kind of wanted someone else to do the cooking. There were plenty of steakhouses off the interstate to choose from. Why would she have any on hand? What she did have on hand was strictly quick-and-easy stuff.

So no steak, ham, sausage, or any other normal breakfast meat. Almost all the regular food she had was pre-cooked and frozen, which would probably taste like rubber to a werewolf. That left only a couple of breakfast-ish options, and from the sound of it, Marla had given up the fight for sleep and was getting dressed now. Adrienne pulled a couple of eggs out of the fridge and set them on the counter. She didn't really have a table to set, considering she didn't do sit-down meals at home. Marla would just have to deal with the lack of domesticity.

The pipes rattled, announcing that Marla had found the bathroom. Adrienne wondered briefly if she was going to do the whole shower bit. That would give her a bit more time, for all the good that was likely to do.

Why did Adrienne care? She should've been hustling the werewolf out the door. It wasn't like one night of admittedly great sex meant anything more than exactly that.

Adrienne poured herself a mug of coffee and chugged it. Then, she poured a second and pulled out a spare mug for Marla.

Marla stepped into the kitchen, eyes bleary and hair obviously finger-combed into something that passed for order. Adrienne mentally gave her points for not assuming she could use the brush hanging in the caddy by the mirror.

"Is that coffee?" Marla asked.

"Yup. Here you go." Adrienne filled her mug and handed it over. "How do you like your eggs?"

"Uh, sunny up, I guess." Marla picked at something on her sleeve, not meeting Adrienne's gaze.

So, as close to raw as possible. Adrienne wouldn't have blinked at just plain raw. It'd be pretty hypocritical if she did. Not that it mattered so long as the eggs were good. Fortunately, they were.

Adrienne made short work of Marla's eggs, handed her the plate and fork, waved her over to a bit of free counter space, and then scrambled up a couple for herself. This was another thing she occasionally got a craving for, and eggs were easy enough, thank whoever. Bread didn't keep well enough to have a loaf on hand for the rare times she might actually want it. She wasn't going to apologize for that, though. She had a feeling Marla wasn't about to miss having toast to dip into her eggs.

Sure enough, Marla dug right in as soon as Adrienne plated her own eggs.

"So, haven't seen you around here before," Adrienne said. "New in town or passing through?"

"New," Marla said. "That obvious?"

"I mean, this isn't a huge town, and I know most of the people who hang out at Darius'."

"Oh." Marla rolled a shoulder as if she were checking something and then looked quickly back down at her plate.

Something about that movement caught Adrienne's attention. At first, she wasn't sure why. Then, she realized that was the same shoulder where she'd noticed the scar.

"Wait a sec," Adrienne said. "Do you mean new-new? As in new to being a werewolf?"

"Yeah." Marla shoveled another chunk of egg into her mouth, probably to avoid saying anything else.

That was understandable, but Adrienne couldn't just let it go at that. She didn't know much about pack law. Darius had explained a few of the basics when he'd helped her adjust after being turned, but what she knew suggested that something was very off about this situation.

"You here to join Darius' pack then?" That made only slightly more sense than already being a member of his pack. Usually when a human agreed to be turned, they were already involved with someone in the pack, generally because they wanted to have kids. Picking up random vampires in the pack alpha's bar would be a really bad idea, if that was the case.

"Hell, no." Marla looked up again. "No pack for me."

Adrienne internally counted to ten, set down her plate, and counted to ten again. A lone wolf in a pack's territory would quickly become a Problem. This woman was new, though. She clearly knew a thing or two, but maybe not that.

"Why not?" she finally asked.

Marla polished off the rest of her eggs and stuck the plate in the sink before answering.

"My ex spouted some 'true mates' bullshit at me when I tried to break up with his abusive ass. Then he turned me."

Adrienne barely kept her jaw from actually dropping in horror.

"Not a great life choice there, giving me super-strength and fangs." Marla gritted her still-human teeth. "Least he won't be doing that to anyone else."

"You killed him?" Not that Marla would be the first person to kill her abuser, but Adrienne really hadn't been expecting that. Among other things, Adrienne hadn't thought she would be able to take on an experienced vampire right when she was first turned. Though, becoming a werewolf didn't involve dying first, so maybe that wasn't a fair comparison. Her mind cycled around that for a bit, trying to process the fact this woman had just dropped this fact so...well, not calmly. Suddenly.

"Wouldn't you?" Marla looked Adrienne directly in the eye.

"I wasn't there," Adrienne said. "But if I thought he was going to kill me, then probably."

Marla gave a curt nod.

"So what about his pack?" Adrienne asked. "I mean, I'm sure they did whatever to keep the human cops out of it, but they just sent you on your way?"

"I didn't stick around to find out." Marla crossed her arms over her chest. "I mean, for all I know, he didn't have a pack."

"I mean, yeah, I guess he could've been a lone wolf. That's pretty rare though. Werewolves are even more social than humans. But the ones I know would never turn someone who wasn't willing." Adrienne scrubbed a hand over her face. "So you don't know if there's a pack hunting you."

"It's been almost a month," Marla said. "I'm not exactly in witness protection. I crossed a couple of state lines, but that doesn't mean much.

If he had a pack and they were looking for me, I'm pretty sure they would've found me by now. Cops too."

"Yeah, maybe. You realize that's all the more reason to join another pack," Adrienne said. "They look out for their own. And I can't speak for all of them, but Darius' pack wouldn't stand for anyone who pulled that shit."

"Didn't come here for life advice."

Maybe not, but it sure seemed like she needed it.

"Look, if nothing else, you should be with other wolves when the moon goes full in a couple of days."

"Not happening. I'll figure something else out." Marla looked her up and down. "Thanks for the lay and the breakfast. I'll see myself out."

The door clicked shut behind her a moment later, leaving Adrienne wondering what, if anything, she needed to do about this.

Marla seemed pretty confident that nobody was chasing her. Werewolf or human, though, murder wasn't usually something that just went away if you ignored it. If her ex had a pack, they'd have handled the legal side of things, but they'd find her eventually. If he didn't, then sooner or later it'd be the cops. Either way, the odds were good that something messy was on its way.

Adrienne sighed and went in search of her phone. Darius deserved to know there could be trouble incoming. Part of her hoped Marla would decide to move on to some other pack's territory. Most of her, against all reason, hoped not.

Chapter 3

Tuesday nights in the emergency room were generally quiet compared to almost any other day of the week, especially the weekends. There'd usually be a kid with a high temp and parents needing to be reassured that the over-the-counter medicine was the same stuff they'd get here. Someone usually came in with injuries from a motor vehicle accident, appendicitis or a gall bladder that needed to come out. Not that she wanted people to be sick or injured, but Adrienne liked to stay busy. Tonight, though, just about anybody who was going to come in already had. Adrienne was not happy she'd let herself be talked into covering for someone out sick. Sure, she was awake all night anyway, but that didn't mean she wanted to be bored while she was.

Some would expect it to get busy just because of the full moon. That wasn't how things worked, though. She'd tracked it for a couple of years to make sure it was an actual pattern at all. Sure enough, people did seem to get more agitated, anxious, or increase any other psychological symptom they had. But it didn't make for more patients, just more interesting ones. So far, she hadn't even seen that tonight. The waiting room was empty, and the folks who'd come in earlier were all in the back or on their way home.

She heard footsteps approaching from the parking lot well before they reached the doors, so she'd already sat up straighter by the time they arrived. They could walk, and they weren't running, so it probably wasn't even going to be an actual emergency.

That thought slipped away as the doors slid open and Marla walked in. For a second, Adrienne lost herself in the memory of Marla's taste and the sound of her sighs. Then Adrienne realized she was cradling an arm that was very obviously broken. The same one that had been bitten.

Marla approached the triage desk and slapped down her driver's license and insurance card with her good hand.

"What the actual hell?" Adrienne hissed.

"What does it look like?" Marla moved her broken arm slightly and winced. "Needed a reason to be here. Didn't know you'd be here too."

So she'd done this to herself?

"It looks like you missed the memo on your healing," Adrienne retorted. "That'll be healed before they even get you to x-ray. Though, if you don't get it set, they'll have to re-break it. They might already have to."

"I know."

"So you want to shift while they're working on it and traumatize some poor doctor? Because, trust me, with pain like that, you won't be in control."

Adrienne glanced at the clock. It was twenty after midnight, though since it was still daylight savings, it wasn't going to truly be midnight for another forty minutes. This newbie werewolf might have been holding off her change just fine for now, focusing on the pain she'd caused herself, but that would not last once the witching hour arrived.

"I thought I wouldn't be able to shift at all if I was under anesthesia. Doesn't it, like, stop everything from working?"

Adrienne closed her eyes and counted to ten, then said, "No. First of all, there's no reason to put you under unless it's way more messed up than it looks. Or, I guess, if they need to re-break it. Second, anesthesia isn't cryostasis. You're just unconscious. There are doctors in most packs, you know. Doctors who actually understand your biology."

That was one of the advantages werewolves had: their pack structures meant they could generally be sure to get everyone's needs met: medical, spiritual, educational, whatever. And if they needed a specialist the pack didn't have? They just reached out to other packs till they found someone. Adrienne thought the fae might have something similar, though they didn't exactly tell outsiders much. She probably wouldn't even know so much about the wolves if not for Darius. They were less secretive than the fae but still didn't exactly broadcast their existence.

Marla had no idea what she was turning away from.

Adrienne picked up the wolf's out of state ID and insurance card and tried to hand them back.

"You can't turn me away, *Adrienne*. There's laws and shit."

"You're stable, so yes, I can. This isn't even the best place for you to get treated. You should be talking to Darius, not me."

Marla wrinkled her nose. Had she even realized the bartender was the pack alpha? Or was it just the general idea of dealing with one?

"Yeah, he's an acquired taste, but he grows on you."

"So does fungus."

Adrienne sighed.

"If I check you in, this is going to be a shit-show. The packs will get involved anyway because they'll need to do damage control."

"That's their problem."

Adrienne leaned in closer. "I thought you didn't want to hurt anyone. Traumatizing people who are happier thinking we're just stories is hurting them. You're damned lucky there's nobody in this waiting room right now. I strongly suggest you turn around, go ask Darius to point you to one of the pack doctors, and get over the idea they're all like your ex."

The look Marla shot her was like a silver stake to Adrienne's heart.

"So you're telling me I can't be treated here?" Marla wasn't quite yelling, but she wasn't not yelling either.

Great. Now Adrienne didn't have much of a choice but to check her in because somebody had probably heard that.

Surprisingly, Marla already had a chart in the system—one that'd be two inches thick if it were paper—so it didn't take long to update her info with her new address. Apparently she'd moved to some corner of town Adrienne had never heard of. Having a chart in the system wasn't that strange, even though it had been surprising. Hospital systems did cross state lines these days, and sometimes their computer systems were even compatible.

She took Marla's vitals. Heart rate and blood pressure were up, but that was probably just a combination of pain and freaking out over whether she was going to change.

Hell, *Adrienne* was freaking out about whether Marla was going to change. From what Darius had told her, werewolves felt a pretty strong compulsion to change during the full moon, but they could override it with practice. That's probably what Marla was doing now, but she was new. Whether she could keep doing it remained to be seen. The full moon was nearly at its peak, and once she got assessed in the ER, Marla would get the good painkillers. What would happen then was anyone's guess. Wonderful.

"All right. Fine. Go back to Nancy, and she'll take you in." Adrienne hit the button to open the door that led to the treatment rooms. Nancy, who'd probably just been waiting for a new chart to pop up on her screen, stood on the other side.

As soon as the doors closed, Adrienne pulled out her phone and shot a text to Darius. If any of the pack doctors had privileges at the hospital, she didn't know about it, but he would. This had the potential to go very, very wrong, and she'd be more damned than she already was if she didn't try to stop it. Hell might or might not be real, but she could sure create one for herself out of guilt. She was very good at that.

⸺◉⸺

Adrienne hated being right sometimes.

"What the hell?" Nancy's shriek carried through the closed doors all the way to triage.

Adrienne groaned. Fortunately, the waiting room was still empty, so she badged herself through the door and followed the growls. Sure enough, Nancy was standing just outside of Room 3, syringe in her shaking hand. Adrienne pushed past her and grabbed the snarling golden-brown wolf by the neck as if she had a collar. Fortunately, Marla's hospital gown was already pooled on the floor, not looped around the wolf's neck. Now, how to explain this fiasco in a way Nancy could handle...

"Goddammit," Adrienne said to the wolf. "I told her you couldn't come back here. How did she even manage to get you in?"

The wolf struggled to get away, but either she wasn't trying, or her foreleg had retained the break when she'd shifted. At this point, Adrienne didn't really care which. She dragged Marla past Nancy and toward the door to the waiting room. Darius was sending a pack doctor according to the last text he'd sent, but they weren't there yet. So, she'd have to improvise.

"But where's my patient?" Nancy asked.

"I dunno, but her dog's going outside," Adrienne said as she elbowed the press-plate to open the doors again. Nancy was going have to reconcile her patient simultaneously leaving against medical advice and smuggling her obviously-not-a-dog in on her own, because Adrienne didn't have any ideas on how to make that make sense.

She tugged the reluctant wolf along with her, through the waiting room and out to the parking lot. She squeezed the key in her pocket with her free hand, and her car's alarm chirped. Too bad employees had to park on the far side. Normally, she didn't give a shit, but normally, she wasn't dragging an oversized "dog" with her. She'd rather security didn't get an eyeful of this and question her about it.

"C'mon," she said, "work with me here."

The wolf wasn't actually struggling anymore, but she was making Adrienne drag her. Whoever the hell Darius was sending, they weren't here yet, and she needed to keep Marla contained until they were. Finally, they got to the car, and Adrienne opened the door to the backseat. Marla jumped in, tongue lolling like a dog excited to go for a drive, golden-green eyes shining brightly.

"*We're* not going anywhere," Adrienne said. "*You* are staying put till the pack rep gets here."

Marla snarled.

"You wanna do something about it?" Adrienne closed the door and reset the alarm. She glared at the wolf. "Give yourself thumbs again."

She turned and went back inside. She hoped Marla would shift back, but given how new she was, that seemed unlikely. The car should keep her contained while she was in wolf form, and Darius' pack-witch had thrown some protections on it too when Adrienne had hired her to ward the apartment. The wards were keyed to Adrienne, but hopefully, if Marla's ex's pack came sniffing around, it'd keep her safe from them too. She didn't have a whole lot of other options.

Nancy was by the triage desk when Adrienne stepped back inside.

"Is she out there?"

"Didn't see her," Adrienne said. "Stuck her dog in my car till we find her. If she doesn't come back for it, I'll bring it to the pound."

"That's...yeah, I guess that makes sense. How did she...?"

"Good question." Adrienne tried to avoid outright lying as much as possible. Much easier to keep track of things that way. "Full moons, right?"

"Yeah." Nancy gave a shaky laugh. "Damn, that dog scared me."

"Yeah." Adrienne was itching to text Darius again to find out what the hell was taking so long. It had only been a few minutes, but it felt like hours.

"I think I'm taking my break early. Need anything from the cafeteria?" Nancy asked.

"I'm good," Adrienne said. Even if she'd still been human, she'd have lost her appetite.

Once Nancy was gone, Adrienne pulled out her phone and saw that Darius had already replied. She cursed when she pulled it up. The doctor he'd been planning to send got called back for a delivery. Of course somebody was giving birth tonight. She replied with a quick explanation of where things stood. Hopefully, they could get to the hospital by the end of her shift. Then it would be their problem.

———◆———

At the end of Adrienne's shift, there was still no sign of anybody from Darius' pack. Fortunately, there wasn't much to pass on in report, so she was able to get out to her car quickly.

Adrienne wasn't sure when she got to her car if it was a good thing or a bad thing that Marla was still in her wolf form. Adrienne had grabbed Marla's belongings for her. She hadn't been sure how well her story about keeping the belongings and dog together would work, but nobody had even asked. So, whenever Marla shifted back, at least she'd have her own clothes.

"Do you even know how to shift back?" Adrienne asked as she tossed the bag of clothes into the backseat with the wolf.

Marla didn't answer.

The drive home was tense. A lot of questions had piled up through the night, none of which Marla could answer in her current state. It was tempting to just drop her with Darius, but she'd made it clear she wanted nothing to do with the pack. Even if Adrienne thought she was wrong, she couldn't make that choice on Marla's behalf.

"I get that it sucks," she found herself saying. "Yeah, insert crappy vampire joke here, but I didn't much want to be turned either. I don't know exactly what you're going through because at least I had a choice. It was a shitty choice, but at least I had one. Your ex was obviously an asshole, and it's just as well you finished him off."

In the rearview mirror, Adrienne saw the wolf tilt her head quizzically.

"Doesn't matter. Just, I get not wanting to be around other werewolves. I don't exactly hang with other vampires. But vamps don't have the kind of support networks that werewolf packs do. The good packs anyway."

Marla lay back down in the back seat. Adrienne hoped that meant she was at least giving some thought to her options.

Why she cared was a whole other question. A few dances and a hookup didn't mean Adrienne owed Marla anything. Her life would be easier if Marla just found somewhere else to move to. Hell, that'd be better for pretty much everyone else in town, considering the possibility of her ex's pack coming around for revenge.

She could chalk it up to her general protectiveness towards patients. This didn't feel quite like that, but it would do for now. She had enough else to focus on.

Adrienne pulled into the garage under her building, parked in her space, and killed the engine. She shot a glance to the backseat.

"You gonna walk in with me or make me drag you again?"

Marla whimpered. Her tail thumped against the seat.

With a roll of her eyes, Adrienne opened the back door and let the wolf out. Marla was even holding her bag in her mouth. Adrienne also noticed she didn't have a limp. Maybe the shift had helped that along.

"Cool." No broken bone meant one less thing to deal with. Adrienne led her up the stairs and unlocked the apartment. Marla went in first, positively answering the question of whether the wards would still recognize her in her wolf form.

Once inside, Marla jumped up on the couch, setting the "belongings bag" down at one end of it.

"Yeah, make yourself at home, I guess," Adrienne said. "Look, I've got to get to sleep. The pack doctor will do what he can to smooth things over at the hospital, I guess. Doesn't look like you need him anymore, so there's no reason he'd come here. You want to hang out here till you shift back, that's fine."

Part of her kind of hoped the werewolf did stay, but she was too tired to worry about it now. She pulled out a tub of beef blood, poured it into her mug, and popped the mug into the microwave. Her supply was running low. She'd have to hit the butcher shop soon.

Marla let out a soft snort followed by a whine.

"Hey, I still gotta eat. Sorry if it stinks." She thought a moment. "Shit. I still don't have any meat or anything. I doubt you want eggs like this."

Another snort. Adrienne decided that was an agreement. She wished she'd thought to hit up a drive-thru on the way home. The microwave dinged, and she pulled out her mug. She sipped at her dinner—or breakfast—as she pulled out her phone and ran a quick search. She didn't have an account with any of the delivery services, but it only took a minute to set one up. The menu options were limited this early in the morning, but frankly, Marla was lucky she was getting anything.

"It's going to be cooked, obviously, but there'll be some breakfast sandwiches here in twenty minutes, if this app can be believed."

Marla whuffed at her.

"I'm gonna finish my dinner and take a shower." Adrienne raised her mug of blood at the wolf in some bizarre toast.

What even was her life?

She was still asking herself that question when she answered the door, hair still wet, and took the bag from the delivery guy. She'd been able to tip through the app, so the fact her wallet was in the other room wasn't a problem. Apps like this hadn't been a thing before she'd been turned, so that had been a pleasant surprise.

"I'm keeping these in the kitchen," she said as she unwrapped the sandwiches and set them on a plate. "So, if you want any, you're gonna have to get off the couch."

By the time she set the plate on the floor, Marla was there, nosing the English muffins away from their contents.

"Figured," Adrienne said. "All right. I'm fading fast. Bon appetit."

It should have been weird, going to sleep with a wolf in the other room. Then again, it should have been weird falling asleep with Marla in her bed the other night. The fact that neither was actually weird was something Adrienne chose not to examine too closely. She was genuinely certain Marla wasn't going to try to kill her in her sleep, not that she'd likely know how, and that was going to have to be good enough.

Chapter 4

When she woke up, Adrienne was surprised to find Marla not only still there, but in human form and making coffee, leaning against the counter next to the machine. The breakfast sandwiches were long gone, the wrappers thrown away, the plate cleaned. All of that was fine. Surprising, but fine.

What was less fine was the frame Marla was holding. Even from the back, Adrienne knew exactly what picture it held, and she wanted to rip it out of Marla's hands and possibly rip out her throat for daring to touch it.

"Who is this?" Marla's eyes glittered dangerously as she straightened, holding up the photo like some kind of smoking gun.

"None of your business." Adrienne grabbed the framed photo, bringing it back into the living room and placing it on the shelf where it belonged. She let herself trace the lines of Monica's wedding dress, eyes lingering on her face. Monica's smile lit up her eyes, their bright blue enhanced by the sapphire gown she'd chosen.

"It is if you used me to cheat on her."

Adrienne swallowed. She didn't owe this werewolf anything. She'd already done more for her than she had any business doing.

"Well?" Marla demanded, arms crossed.

"I didn't use you to cheat on her," Adrienne said.

"No? Pretty sure most people don't keep their wedding photos with their ex on a shelf after they get divorced."

"Till death do us part may not cover undeath, but only one person has to die for the marriage to be over."

"Oh, shit."

A part of Adrienne was pleased at the guilt in Marla's voice. Another part of her felt she'd just cut away another of the remaining bits of her humanity. Had she really just used Monica like a weapon? She stepped back from the photo, which suddenly felt as if her touch and her words had soiled it.

"I'm sorry."

"You didn't know." Adrienne went back to the kitchen and grabbed a mug. Not wanting to wait for the coffee to finish brewing, she pulled the pot away and stuck the mug under the stream of liquid. For good measure, she poured some in from the pot at the same time. She set the pot back in its place without losing a drop, then quickly drained the mug.

After peering in the fridge, she grabbed the tub of pig's blood, refilled her mug with it, and then popped her mug in the microwave.

"How do you do it?" Marla asked.

"Do what? Drink blood? Keep going?" Adrienne cut herself off. "You're gonna have to be more specific."

"How the hell are you a nurse?" Marla asked. "People must come into that ER bleeding all the time."

Adrienne turned to stare at her. *That* was her question?

"One, I don't usually work in the ER. Two, I haven't had human blood since I was turned, and frankly, even that doesn't count. The one who turned me was obviously a vampire. Three, I don't go to work hungry. Ever. Four, was I supposed to learn a new job just because I'm undead now? Hell, nobody else actually *wants* night shift. I sure didn't when I was human."

Marla didn't say anything, but she leaned back against the counter again. She slouched in on herself a bit and her hair fell forward, half-hiding her face. Adrienne stopped herself from reaching over to brush it away, though her fingers remembered the silky feel.

"Why are you even still here? I figured you'd have hit the road long before I woke up." The microwave dinged, and Marla pulled out her mug.

"I was going to."

"And?" Adrienne took a long sip of blood.

"And someone was in the hall. Someone who smelled kind of like Eddie. A couple of them."

After setting the mug down, Adrienne took a long, cautious breath, sampling the air in and near the apartment. Sure enough, Marla's wasn't the only werewolf scent, and the others weren't familiar. They were fainter and had probably been gone for hours. They hadn't gotten in, though whether that was due to the wards or lack of trying, Adrienne couldn't be sure. They might still be down in the parking garage or something.

Shit.

She checked her phone. No more messages from Darius.

"You couldn't have, I don't know, led with that? I'm going to have to tell the pack," Adrienne said. This was getting out of hand. "All I told them last night was a non-pack werewolf had showed up injured. I didn't even tell them you were the same one from the other night, though I have a feeling Darius guessed. But if your ex's pack is actually here hunting you, the local pack needs to know."

"Bullshit. This is my problem, not theirs!" Marla snapped.

"This could turn into a full-on war. You get that, right? Even if you left right now, Darius' pack has been harboring you as far as they're concerned."

"That's ridiculous! They don't even know I'm here," Marla snapped, glaring up at Adrienne from behind the hair still hanging in her face. "Sounds like these packs just look for a reason to fight."

"Some do," Adrienne said. "Considering what an asshole your late ex was, it wouldn't surprise me if his is like that. You could use the help of a pack with a little more integrity."

"Not all packs?" Marla scoffed. "Heard that before, all kinds of ways."

There was no good answer for that. Rather than try, she fired off a text to Darius. Then she drained her mug, pulled a tub of blood from the fridge, didn't even bother to look at which kind it was, refilled the mug, and popped it in the microwave. She needed to think. No matter how she played this, it was a Situation now, and she was smack in the middle of it.

The microwave dinged, and she grabbed her mug, taking it with her back to the bedroom. She made sure the door was well shut, then took a long swallow of blood. Her fangs weren't useful for drinking blood this way, but they pushed to be let free anyway. Usually, she suppressed the urge. This time, she let them slide into place. Then, she pulled up the scheduling office number in her phone.

———◉———

"What, you thought I wasn't going to hear you calling out sick?" Marla asked when Adrienne came back out to the kitchen, fangs firmly retracted.

"Obviously not. Your hearing's at least as good as mine. Didn't want background noise is all," Adrienne snapped. "So, what can you tell me about your ex's pack?"

"I told you, I don't know them," Marla said. "I didn't even know he was a werewolf till he turned me."

"Yeah, but he must've had friends or something. Drinking buddies?" Marla laughed bitterly.

"If he did, I never saw them. I went to work, came home, and that was it. We never went anywhere and never had anyone over. He didn't even much like me having a job."

"Damn." Well, that was no help. "Okay, so we're working off scents and not much else. Awesome."

"We?"

Adrienne looked over at Marla. She was still curled in on herself, arms protectively crossed over her midsection. That wasn't going to work.

"Yeah, we. Like it or not, we've got to deal with this. If nothing else, we've got to get out of here before any of my clueless human neighbors get tangled up in whatever the hell this is. I know you'd rather go back to whatever your life was before you met that piece of shit."

"Gee, ya think?"

"Fuck knows, I'd rather go back to ..."

An image of Monica flashed through her mind. She was smiling, one hand over her belly, the other reaching toward the ultrasound screen. Adrienne cut the scene short there. Before the explosion. Before...everything.

"But I can't go back," she continued. "Neither can you. There are literal wolves out there hunting you, but you're a pretty badass wolf yourself."

Marla just stared at her, eyes wide.

"Don't look at me like that! You wouldn't even be here if that weren't true. So, are you gonna hide up in here feeling sorry for yourself? Or are you gonna step up?"

"What does that even mean?" Marla demanded. She straightened a bit, arms still crossed, but now over her chest.

Adrienne's phone buzzed in her pocket. She pulled it out and read Darius' text. She grinned.

"It means they think they're setting a trap for you, but we've got the home field advantage."

⸺◦⸺

The plan was simple enough. Adrienne liked simple. Fewer moving parts meant fewer potential mistakes. Something still would go wrong, of course. No way around that. No plan could survive first contact with the enemy. The trick was to put that off as long as possible.

Step one: get away from the civilians. This building had a ton of humans who had no idea werewolves were even a thing. That wouldn't keep them safe if the creatures Adrienne had spotted out front decided to attack.

"There are two out front, and odds are, there are a couple in the parking garage," Adrienne said. "Probably the back exit too."

"So, what, we're going through the sewers or something?"

"Ew, no." The very idea of sloshing through a sewer made Adrienne want to puke. If she even still could puke. She hadn't tested that yet and didn't really want to do so now. "How's your arm?"

Marla held up her arm. It looked like it had never been broken.

"Right, it's terrible. Turns out it was a compound fracture, and since you left against medical advice, it got infected," Adrienne said, voice dripping with as much sarcasm as she could pour into it.

"Uh, what now?"

"So that doctor that was going to come check you over last night is sending us an ambulance." Adrienne plowed ahead. "The paramedics are fae, so while the wolves out there will know they're not human, they won't be sure they're not coming into the building for a human patient."

"And then they're going to, what, teleport us out of here?"

Adrienne really, really wished that was an option, but if any of the fae could teleport, she didn't know about it.

"No, but if you stop interrupting, I can explain."

Finally, Marla shut up and let Adrienne talk.

<hr>

The fae paramedics did a legit check of Marla's arm once Adrienne convinced the wards to let them inside. They'd made a good show of their entrance, complete with big flashy red cardiac bag and stretcher. Adrienne probably should've given that arm more than a visual once-over, but she hadn't really trusted herself to touch Marla right now. Part of her was annoyed enough to want to shake her. That and, as much as she didn't want to admit it and was putting on her best, "I'm the nurse, so I know what's going on here" face, she was worried. Worried about the impact on Darius' pack and everyone else getting dragged into this, yes, but also worried about Marla. There wasn't time for that or for worrying about what that meant for her.

"Looks good," said the one with electric blue hair and eyes to match. "Too good. That's okay, though. We can work it into the spell."

"Spell?" Marla looked no happier about that now than she had been when Adrienne had explained the plan. She did let them start wrapping her arm up into a sling.

Adrienne got it. She did. Living in a world where magic and monsters were real was weird for the first year or so after getting turned. Fae spells were uncomfortable too. She might have left that bit out of the explanation.

"Ouch! Watch it!"

The paramedics both kept up their chant, which sounded like it was probably Gaelic or something. As she watched, Adrienne saw Marla's skin turn grayish. Meanwhile, the air was growing thick with a putrid odor.

"Ugh," Adrienne said. "Why'd you pick that one? Who the hell gets C. diff in a broken arm?"

"You know anything more likely to keep everyone away?" asked the less-obviously fae paramedic, expression innocently bland. "Humans, yes, but especially wolves?"

Clostridium difficile was pretty much the worst diarrhea short of cholera, and while Adrienne had never smelled cholera, she had to agree that the smell of this particular bacterium was horrific. It made her gag and, frankly, the stench might have more to do with how sick Marla was looking than the visual component of the spell.

"Fair enough," she agreed. "Can we hit the road now?"

"Fair enough?" Marla asked.

The paramedics got the werewolf onto the stretcher, but she balked when they tried to buckle her in.

"It's just a safety-"

"You are not belting me down on this thing!"

"Hey!"

Everyone turned to look at Adrienne. She didn't like using her vampire powers, especially her vocal compulsion. Stealing someone's will was worse than killing them, as far as Adrienne was concerned. That was a line she'd so far held firmly ever since she'd discovered it. Other nurses might think they wanted to be able to force their patients to do what they needed to do, but the one time Adrienne had accidentally done so, she'd been horrified.

This was a different situation, though. They needed to get moving and there wasn't exactly time for an argument. She stepped closer to the stretcher and Marla glared up at her. Adrienne closed her eyes for a moment and reeled the compulsion back in. Stopping the argument was one thing, but she didn't want to actually force Marla to cooperate if she could avoid it. It felt gross enough that she'd compelled her at all.

"If I wanted to hand you over to them, all I'd have had to do is open the door."

Marla's glare wavered.

"I need you to trust me," Adrienne said softly, willing Marla to see that Adrienne was on her side. "I won't *make* you trust me. But I need you to. Just a little longer."

After a moment, Marla nodded. Then they were out the door and down the stairs, wards hastily reset.

Chapter 5

The ambulance ride to Darius' was nothing like the last time Adrienne had ridden in one. The memories cascaded over her anyway.

"Hang another unit of o-neg!"

Cold fingers on her wrist. Ringing in her ears. Eyes can't focus.

"It's not enough. She's gotta be bleeding internally."

"Monica?" Adrienne asked.

EMT face in the haze. Familiar? Sharp features. Eyes a strange reddish-brown.

"She's in one of the other ambulances. They're doing everything they can for her. Just like we're doing for you."

Pain.

Explosion.

Chaos.

"Hey, look at me."

Blink.

"You've got internal bleeding somewhere. We're giving you blood, but you're losing it somewhere as fast as we can put it in."

Fuck.

Monica? Baby?

"I don't know, but they're doing everything they can for her."

Terror.

"There is something I can do," the paramedic whispered next to Adrienne's ear. "The fact you're losing blood so fast...it complicates some stuff but would make this bit easier."

What?

"I'm not sure we can keep you alive as you are. But if you have just a bit of my blood...it wouldn't be the same life, but you'd still be there for Monica."

Runbadno! Trapped!

"I won't force you. But it may be the only chance I can offer you."

In the end, she drank. She couldn't bear the thought of Monica alone. If she lost the pregnancy, it would be two blows at once. Adrienne had to be there for her, no matter what. As the coppery liquid flowed down her throat it felt like it was filling every cell in her body. She felt strong. Like anything was possible. Whatever happened, she'd be there to help Monica through it.

But Monica wouldn't be there to help her.

"Hey, where'd you go?" Marla asked.

The sirens had cut out, and the fae paramedics had some kind of folk music playing on the radio. It was bright and cheerful and was probably meant to be soothing. Instead, Adrienne's nerves were vibrating in tune with every spritely note being played on the acoustic guitar.

Marla had long since gotten off the stretcher and was sitting across from Adrienne. She rested a hand on Adrienne's forearm and peered up at her. She looked more like the woman Adrienne remembered from the other night, unsure if she was welcome. Her touch set off sparks of memories that were much more enjoyable, but Adrienne couldn't get lost in those either. Not the time.

"Just thinking. I hope Darius has more of a plan by the time we get there."

"I thought the whole point was there was a plan?" Marla sat back, taking the warmth of her hand with her.

"There was a plan to get civilians out of the line of fire," Adrienne said. "Other than that, the plan is mostly 'don't get dead.'"

"Great plan."

Adrienne pulled out her phone and checked it. No updates. Between the illusions and the ambulance, they had a decent lead on the wolves. If they'd done their homework, though, they wouldn't be far behind.

If there weren't scouts ahead of them.

When they arrived at the small campground Darius had taken over a few years back, there were too many wolf scents for Adrienne to be sure if all of them were Darius' pack or not. It'd be useful if they had some kind of common note, but that would make life too easy. All she could smell was a cacophony of "wolf," drowning out even the scent of the pine trees that dominated the area.

"Let's go." One of the fae paramedics swung the back door of the ambulance open. "Before the other wolves get here."

Marla jumped down to the gravel that coated the lot. Her posture straightened and her jaw set as she clearly prepared herself for a fight. For a second, Adrienne thought the werewolf might shift and bolt. Adrienne could only imagine how she felt. As scary as her first months as a vampire had been, they hadn't included being pursued for murder, and she'd had Darius to at least somewhat show her the ropes. The thought of Marla being on the run on her own hurt.

Adrienne stepped out of the ambulance and stood beside Marla. Somewhere overhead, a mourning dove cooed.

That wasn't ominous at all.

"C'mon," Adrienne said. "Let's at least get you introduced before shit hits the fan."

Marla's already squared-off shoulders stiffened, but she nodded and followed Adrienne over to where Darius stood with a couple of pack members. One was the grumpy shot boy, who looked like he was ready to throw hands at anyone who so much as looked at his alpha the wrong way. Another was someone Adrienne had never met. The rest were presumably in various cabins or in the woods surrounding the campground.

"Wait, you? The goofy bartender?" Marla asked with a choked sort of laugh.

Adrienne hadn't realized Marla hadn't put that together already.

"Yeah, me. Good to meet you." Darius stuck his hand out. "I mean, I kinda met you the other night, but all I got was 'Somethin' Punkin,' which I'm guessing isn't your name. I'm Darius MacGearailt, alpha of the Southeast Connecticut Pack."

He didn't introduce the wolves next to him, just waited with that goofy grin of his for Marla to shake his hand. Marla held back at first, expression wary. Then she set her jaw and shook his hand.

"Marla Smith," she said.

Darius raised an eyebrow at the generic-sounding last name but didn't comment.

"I don't know your whole story," Darius said. "You don't owe it to me. Adrienne vouched for you, which was enough to get you here. But if my pack is going to be taking risks to protect you, I want your word too."

"My word for what?"

"I need to know that they're not hunting you because you hurt or killed one of their pack mates."

Fuck. Adrienne had managed to tap-dance around any specifics, but that was pretty direct. She hoped Marla had more sense than to lie.

The two wolves stared at each other for a long moment.

"Adrienne tells me you don't approve of turning people against their will," Marla said at last.

"Absolutely not." Darius looked furious. "You telling me one of these wolves turned you without your consent?"

Marla's posture got impossibly stiffer. "I already dealt with the one who changed me. He won't be turning anyone else. I think this is his pack."

Darius' jaw set. Adrienne wondered which way he'd go. She was still pretty sure he'd take Marla in, but pack law was weird. He might even say this asshole's pack was within their rights to avenge him or something.

In her head, Adrienne mapped out an escape route. She could probably get Marla at least to the river, maybe even to a ferry. Getting across water was one of the best ways to break a scent trail, even if it was also a pretty obvious one. With all the ferries out of New London, Marla's pursuers would have four islands to search, which would split them up and slow them down.

When had she made Marla her cause? Somewhere between breaking her own arm to get out of shifting and when she'd broken Adrienne out of her flashback, Marla had become something more than just someone she'd picked up for a good time. At a minimum, she The thought sent a shiver down Adrienne's spine, and she wasn't sure how much was sense memory of Marla's nails digging into her back and how much was fear. There wasn't time to sort that out now.

"That's messy," Darius said at last. "We've already helped you escape them once, so we have a responsibility to see this through. Get inside one of the cabins for now, but be ready to shift if this gets violent. We'll fight with you, not for you."

"*If* this gets violent? What do you think they-?"

Adrienne breathed a sigh of relief and dragged Marla, still sputtering, toward the nearest cabin, hoping it was empty.

⊸◉⊸

"What the hell does that even mean?" Marla demanded, pacing the length of the cabin's main room.

Adrienne hadn't ever been to Darius' pack territory before. She'd assumed the cabins would be pretty rustic but was pleasantly surprised to find they had electricity and running water. WiFi was a bit lacking, but that wasn't a big priority right now. For now, she just sank further and further into the green and gold sofa that looked like it had escaped the 1970s. Its rough texture grounded her, settling her earlier fears a little.

"Look, I don't understand pack politics," Adrienne said. "I may be friends with Darius, but I'm still an outsider."

"So, I have the pack's protection, but if there's violence, I need to fight. Well, no shit I need to fight! It's my fight! What did you tell them when you called for help anyway?"

Adrienne counted to ten. Twice.

Marla paced.

"I told them you were being hunted. I told them you were newly turned and not from around here. That's it."

"But if I'm supposed to fight, why am I not out there right now? None of this makes any sense!" Marla reached the far wall, turned, and stalked back. Now, she was more like a ping-pong ball of anger and fear than the graceful dancer Adrienne had first met. There was still some of that deliberation in her movement, though, as if each step was carefully planned despite how quickly she was moving. The effect was dizzying.

"Darius is not big into violence. You might have noticed the anti-violence wards on the club?"

"The what?"

Adrienne ran her fingers through her hair. Of course, Marla hadn't. She had no idea what to look for. How would she? There was so much Marla needed to know about this world, most of which Darius had taught Adrienne. It wasn't reasonable to think Adrienne could have gotten Marla up to speed in the little time they'd had, but she still felt like she was failing.

"When you came through the door, did you notice a kind of tingly sensation? Like you just walked through a beaded curtain that wasn't there and got little electric shocks off the beads?"

"Uh, maybe?"

"Darius has a contract with a witch who keeps wards on the place. No violence possible in there."

"Then why not just have something like that here?"

"Because a couple of hours inside those wards is fine," Adrienne said. "But you can't have that where you live. Not if you're a predator. That's really not a good idea for any of us."

Adrienne remembered asking Darius the same thing. His answer had been to make her spend an entire day at the bar. It had been torture after the first few hours, like listening to an off-key lullabye. Even if she didn't actually need to hunt, even if store-bought animal blood would satiate her hunger, the continuous calming effect of the spells was too contrary to her nature.

Also, if there had been some kind of wards set to keep non-pack members out, Darius wouldn't have been able to tweak them to let in an unfamiliar wolf, two fae, and a vampire without just dropping them entirely. So, either he didn't have them at all, or they were down. No reason to go into the finer points of warding with Marla until later.

If there was a later.

"So, what does that mean? He's just going to wait and see if they attack? Because trust me, they're going to."

"Like I said, pack politics aren't my thing," Adrienne said. She was starting to get really annoyed with herself for not learning more, even though she could never be pack. "But my guess is he'll try to get their alpha to talk first. Maybe he doesn't know what your ex did. Or, if he's outnumbered by the local pack, maybe he can pretend he didn't know in order to save face. I don't know. You're probably-"

The sound of engines had both of them running to the window. Two large silver SUVs were just coming to a stop about a hundred yards away. Darius was standing outside to greet them, flanked by the same two wolves as before. Four other wolves poured out of the first SUV, three men and one woman. They were all wearing suits that made Adrienne think of bodyguards flanking a celebrity. The one who was clearly the celebrity in this scenario was tall, pale, and muscular. They approached Darius.

"Can you hear them?" Marla asked. "They're, like, just out of my range."

"They shouldn't be." Adrienne concentrated. She could hear their heartbeats, which were fast and getting faster, but not what they were saying. She wondered if that was some other kind of spell, maybe attached to an object. Maybe one that Darius was wearing or carrying? Must be, otherwise how would he control where it was effective? She gave herself a mental shake. Time enough to wonder about that later. "I can't hear them either."

The tall, pale guy speaking to Darius was probably the alpha. As far as Adrienne knew, alphas weren't always guys, but more than half the time they were. Most packs went for physical strength when they selected their alphas, and that generally favored the men. Darius wasn't exactly short, but he also wasn't as physically imposing as this other fellow. Adrienne was willing to bet his pack had chosen him for his smarts, his personality, or both, not his physicality. She hoped that would pay off now.

One of the wolves with the other alpha was clearly not happy with how things were going. She pushed her way between the alpha and the woman who was probably his second. Adrienne could hear her heart bounding practically in time with her furious gestures.

Marla was nearly vibrating out of her skin, though whether with fear or anger, Adrienne couldn't tell. Probably both.

"Oh, screw this." Marla slammed the door open and stalked out to join the quickly disintegrating parley.

Realistically, Adrienne knew she had already done enough and then some for this person she'd known for less than a week. A one-night stand, an ER visit, and a couple of breakfasts did not mean she needed to get into the middle of some werewolf inter-pack bullshit. She shouldn't have even stayed once they'd gotten Marla here. She could've left with the fae paramedics. Should have, really. Why hadn't she?

The angry woman turned toward Marla and lunged. The alpha held her back, barely. Darius looked over to see that Marla had ignored his orders and threw his hands up in the air.

No, she couldn't have left, dammit. Adrienne raced out the door to catch up.

"You are all guests here," Darius was saying as Adrienne finally got within range. "We were having a reasonable conversation."

"This little slut seduced my sweet Eddie and then killed him!" the woman shrieked. "Now she's got you under her spell too."

"Trust me when I say I'm not under anybody's spell," Darius said.

"Bitch, your son had me under his thumb for months," Marla said. "Did your sweet Eddie even tell you I existed?"

"You lie," the woman retorted. "I would have known if he was seeing anyone."

One of the other werewolves took over restraining her. The alpha turned to size up Marla.

"So he'd been a monk for like half a year?" Marla snorted. "Yeah, right. He'd never last that long."

"Is it true that he turned you without your consent?" the other alpha asked.

Adrienne stopped short when Darius glared at her, clearly not wanting her any closer. She didn't like it. So far, it was still just yelling. If these were family members on her floor at the hospital, she'd know what to do. Hell, she'd had to break up enough loud arguments that would be downright comfy to deal with. But here? Where she had no real role? If she had to stay a couple of steps back, well, fine, but she wouldn't like it.

"Yes," Marla said. "After spending months beating the crap out of me if I took too long to get home from work or called my mother, he decided the way to make me an obedient little girlfriend was to turn me. I didn't even know he *was* a werewolf before that."

"Liar!"

Adrienne clenched her fists and scanned the werewolves. They were edgy, but other than Eddie's mother, they weren't ready to go off. Then, she caught movement off to the side in the other SUV.

"Darius," she murmured.

"I see," he replied.

More werewolves climbed out of the SUV and stood in a semicircle around their alpha. They were less well-dressed than the first crew. Their jeans and flannel shirts made them look like the muscle of the bodyguard contingent. That was probably true. Aside from the bereaved mother and the one holding her back, the rest stood in loose fighting stances. Were they planning to do this in human form? Surely not.

"She's telling the truth," the other alpha said. "You know you'd smell the lie otherwise, Carol."

"That changes nothing!" the bereaved mother shouted. "She still killed my Eddie! She's not even trying to deny it!"

"I'm not denying shit," Marla said. "I killed the son of a bitch that beat me and stole my humanity. What does it matter why he did it?"

"Does what matter, whelp?" the other alpha asked.

"Does it matter what he did?" Marla demanded. "Does it matter why I killed him?"

"I mean, it still doesn't exactly sound like self-defense," one of the other wolves said. "You could've just run away."

Darius growled but said nothing. A couple of his packmates took deliberate steps forward, closer to both Darius and Marla.

"You think I didn't-" Marla snapped her mouth shut.

Adrienne's nails had turned to claws and were now digging into her palms. She'd heard a few too many versions of that bullshit before. As if most people who were killed by their abusers weren't killed exactly when they tried to get away. And that was without factoring in an abuser with werewolf strength and hunting abilities.

Carol's growls had been slowly growing louder. Suddenly, either the person restraining her let go or she broke free, lunging for Marla and shifting into wolf form as she leapt. The other wolves tore off their clothes and shifted as well but made no move beyond that.

Marla shifted too, but either her injury was still affecting her or she was just too new, making her slower. Carol sank her teeth into Marla's shoulder before her fur was in place to protect her. Blood spurted from the wound, filling Adrienne's nose with rich copper, overwhelming all the other wolf scents, and tinging her vision with red.

To her left, Darius jumped the other alpha, but Adrienne couldn't focus on him. Her fangs slid into place, and she was on Carol in two steps, claws digging into her fur and pulling her off Marla, who let out a growl. The next thing Adrienne knew, there were three more wolves on top of them. At least one was one of Darius'. Two were trying to drag Adrienne back, and they succeeded in getting Carol free, dislocating Adrienne's shoulder in the process, costing her precious time to force it back into place. The rest were on Marla, Carol joining them. More blood filled the air, and it was almost all Marla's. Adrienne screamed as her chest tightened in fear.

Not again.

She dug her fangs into the muzzle of the wolf who hung off her arm and kicked away the one on her leg. The blood that filled her mouth darkened her vision further, casting sharp shadows of red over everything. Then, she began to pull at the pile of wolves hiding Marla from her view. There were too many, and the last one she'd yanked off of Marla had taken a chunk of her with him.

"STOP!" she shouted, putting every bit of compulsion into it she could. "All of you stop fighting, NOW!"

Silence fell. All the wolves froze and looked at her, shock written over their faces.

She pushed through the mass of fur and muscle on top of Marla, tossing the now-docile werewolves aside as she went, and knelt. Marla was bleeding from too many places, and her respirations were shallow and rapid. Adrienne had no idea what a normal respiratory rate was for a werewolf in wolf form, but she was pretty sure this wasn't it. Marla's body was desperately fighting for oxygen. Adrienne ripped off her jacket and started tearing it into strips as if it were gauze, binding the wounds where she could, packing them everywhere else.

It wasn't going to be enough.

"Get the pack doctor," she ordered. "I need help stabilizing her."

One of the gray wolves shifted back to human form, took a step towards her, then stopped and looked to Darius, who had shifted back as well. A corner of her brain registered that they were naked and not exactly rushing to get their clothes back on. Were they expecting to need to shift again?

"You don't give the orders here, vampire," Darius said.

"Please," Adrienne forced through gritted teeth, "can you call in the pack doctor to help stabilize her?"

The two alphas stared at each other for a moment. The visiting alpha gave a slight nod. Darius echoed the movement, and the next thing Adrienne knew, the doctor was at her side.

"Can you keep pressure on that abdominal wound and bring her to that cabin? If not I can grab my bag, but-"

Adrienne didn't pay any attention to the rest of what he said. She scooped Marla into her arms and ran.

Chapter 6

Even after they had Marla stitched and washed up, she still looked horrible. Adrienne had to admit that Ty, the pack doctor, did a good job with Marla's stitches. Even if she were human, the wounds would likely have healed without a scar. Her breaths were still shallow and rapid, though, and her heart was beating like a hummingbird's. Her gums were pale but not blue.

"She needs blood," Adrienne said. Again. Adrienne did too, for that matter, and it was taking every ounce of control she had to resist the scent of blood that permeated the room. It was all fresh blood, though, whether Marla's or anyone else's. Ty had done what he could to minimize it, but it was impossible to remove all of it from Marla's fur without disturbing the freshly-sealed wound.

"I don't exactly stock it," Ty snapped. "If I did, you'd know it. And don't get any crazy ideas about giving her yours."

"If I was going to turn someone, it wouldn't be without their permission, and it sure as shit wouldn't be someone who'd already been turned into a werewolf!"

Ty held up his hands. "You're not thinking, vampire. By the time I got a couple units of o-neg here, she wouldn't need it anymore."

He was right, and she knew it. There was nothing left that Adrienne could do.

"What happens now?" she asked. "They're not going to just give up and go home. Carol won't be satisfied until Marla's dead."

"Darius and Peter are probably negotiating something. You were right. Nothing about that fight was as it should have been. There's a way things are supposed to be done, and that wasn't it."

As far as Adrienne was concerned, the fight just shouldn't have *been* at all. She fought the urge to stroke the light gold fur on Marla's head. She wasn't a dog, for fuck's sake. Instead, Adrienne made another sweep of the small clinic office and found one whole alcohol pad that was still sealed and hadn't been put away. She tucked it into its spot in one of the drawers and closed the drawer with a click. Nothing else left to do.

She sat down again next to the exam table where Marla was sleeping. She was glad Marla was still in her wolf form. Even breathing as quickly as she was, this was too similar to when she'd been brought in to see Monica...after.

"I'm going to go check in on the Ortizes," Ty said, grabbing his medical bag. "Babies tend to pick up when something's going on, and they're first-time parents."

Adrienne nodded, not taking her eyes off Marla.

"If she wakes up, try to convince her to stay in wolf form until she doesn't need those butterflies," he said.

Adrienne nodded again. That was something she hadn't considered. Marla's arm had definitely seemed to heal faster when she was in wolf form. Would it have regressed if she'd shifted back sooner than she did? Changing size and shape was an obvious way to tear wounds back open. Did the moon still have an effect the night after the full? And if so, would it be a help or a hindrance? So much she didn't know. Why hadn't she asked these questions before? These were things a nurse living in an area with a werewolf pack should know.

Marla stirred, eyes blinking open owlishly. She tried to lift her head but then set it back down right away with a whine.

"Don't try to get up," Adrienne said. "And don't shift. Doctor's orders."

That earned her a glare that had her raising her hands in surrender.

"Doctor's orders," she repeated. "Not nurse's. You've got a lot of wounds, and some of them are pretty deep. He used dissolving stitches for the internal stuff, but he said to stay in wolf form till the surface stuff had healed. He'll be back soon."

He'd better be. If those other werewolves tried to storm the clinic, Adrienne could hold them off for a while, but she didn't like the odds of them them piling on her like they had on Marla. She could try to command them again, but now, they'd be ready for it. Darius and the other alpha were powerful enough in their own right that they could probably outright ignore her. She wasn't sure about the rest.

"If you were in human form, I'd be offering you crushed ice. Not sure how well that'll work now, but we can give it a shot if Ty has any around here."

She opened the small fridge labeled "food." There were a couple of cuts of meat thawing in the refrigerator portion. The freezer had a tiny tray of ice cubes, which she pulled out and dumped into a clean cloth. There was no sign of a mortar and pestle or anything else useful, so she just slammed her fist down on the bundle of ice. The crunch as it broke was kind of therapeutic, as was the sting of the impact.

Marla gave a little yip of surprise.

"Sorry. Gonna have to do that another time or two to get these smaller."

The door to the cabin clicked open.

"That would've worked better if you'd left them whole," Ty said.

Of course it would have.

She scooped some of the smashed ice into her hand and set it next to Marla's mouth. The wolf hesitated at first, then darted her tongue out to take some of the small pieces. It would be the most natural thing in the world to smooth the fur between her ears as she did, but Adrienne wasn't sure how that would go over.

"Not too much," Adrienne said. "Let it melt in your mouth."

Marla just swallowed, because of course she did.

"What is this, opposite day?"

"She'll be okay," Ty said. He'd stepped closer and was pulling back her dressings to check how the wounds were healing. It had been maybe half an hour, which was even faster than Adrienne would have thought possible. "If that abdominal wound had been any deeper, maybe not, but it's nearly healed."

Marla whuffed.

"He said *nearly*." Adrienne nudged Marla's snout with the ice until she took a bit more. "You heal faster in this form, but not that damn fast."

"Soon as they've healed over completely, you should be fine," Ty said. "You're new, though, so if the skin isn't all the way sealed, it might tear worse when you change. With more time and practice, that won't be as big a problem."

Another whine.

This time Adrienne gave in to temptation and smoothed her empty hand over the fur of Marla's head, one of the few places she'd managed not to get hurt. It wasn't silky like her hair, but it was soft and smooth. She hoped Marla would get the chance to learn more control over her changes, the chance to really be who she was in both forms. That was just her nurse instincts though. She'd wish the same or similar for any of her patients as they recovered, right?

She looked into Marla's golden eyes and knew she was full of shit.

⁎ ⁎ ⁎

By the time Darius came to talk to them, Marla was back in her human form and wearing what was left of her clothes. She hadn't said much other than to answer Ty's questions as he'd checked her over. Adrienne tried not to take that personally. He'd prescribed her a very rare steak and proceeded to throw one on the grill just as Darius arrived.

Adrienne did not like the look on his face. The Darius she knew sported a goofy grin ninety-nine percent of the time. He no longer looked furious as he had earlier, but his mouth was set in a tight line. That was somehow worse.

He came into the cabin and focused immediately on Marla.

"How are you doing?"

Marla shrugged but didn't say anything.

"What happens now?" Adrienne asked.

"I managed to get Peter to agree to give you a day to recover," he said to Marla. "He agrees his pack was out of line to swarm you like that."

Adrienne scoffed.

"And you were out of line getting involved at all," he continued.

"What? If I hadn't, Marla would be dead right now!"

"I know." Darius held up his hands. "Doesn't change pack law."

Adrienne had a few choice things to say about pack law, but she kept them to herself.

"One day and then what?" Marla snapped.

Ty came back into the now-crowded medical cabin with a barely-seared steak smelling richly of blood, which he plunked down on the over-bed table next to where Marla was perched. He adjusted the height and handed her some presumably non-silver flatware. Adrienne could smell the barely-warmed blood seeping from it, suddenly very aware that it had been several hours since she'd eaten. It was probably getting close to dawn.

Marla held back for a moment, then dug in.

"And then what?" Adrienne echoed, focusing on the logistics and trying to ignore the insistent pull to feed.

"Then Marla and Carol fight." Darius raised his hands and turned to look at Marla. "One on one! You do admit to killing her son, and even if I believe your reasons and that you were justified, there's no way to prove any of it."

Adrienne thought about the records she'd seen when she'd checked Marla in to the ER. She hadn't gone digging, but she was willing to bet they'd show a history of injuries with mysterious causes. Each one probably ended with, "Patient screened for intimate partner violence. Reports feeling safe at home." That part wouldn't help, but the rest could.

It would take a subpoena to get them, though, and clearly the pack was not about to wait around for human justice to run its course.

Hell, Adrienne didn't want to think about whether or not the police were even looking for Eddie. One problem at a time.

Marla speared a chunk of steak on her fork and looked at it as she asked, "It's to the death, isn't it?"

"Yeah," Darius said. "That's ..."

"Pack law," Marla finished.

"Pack law sucks," Adrienne said.

"Pack law keeps us from constantly being at each other's throats," Darius said. "We're predators. Our laws keep the violence among us contained."

"Didn't stop Eddie from beating the crap out of me," Marla said around another mouthful of steak. "Didn't stop him from turning me when he found out..."

"What?" Darius asked when she didn't finish.

"I got pregnant," she said, looking down and pushing the last bits of steak around her plate. "I think maybe he switched out some of my pills. Or maybe they just failed. Whatever."

Adrienne winced at that. This just kept getting worse. If Marla hadn't already killed this asshole, Adrienne would have had to.

"I wasn't about to bring a kid into that situation," Marla continued. "I was trying to figure out how to leave him, but it was going to take time. I knew he'd come after me, so I got an abortion."

"And that's when he turned you?"

Marla nodded.

"Does any of that help her case?" Adrienne asked. "You must have pack lawyers who'd know how to get ahold of her medical records."

"It wouldn't make a difference," Ty said. "All it would show was that you terminated the pregnancy, Marla. Unless you told them why and they documented it?"

Marla shook her head.

Damn.

"How is this any better than the bullshit that passes for a legal system in the human world?" Adrienne demanded.

"Didn't say it was better," Darius said. "Just said it's what we've got."

Marla pushed her plate away with a huff and looked up at Ty.

"Could you two please give us a moment?" she asked.

Well, that didn't sound ominous at all.

Ty looked to Darius, who nodded. Both men left the cabin, which suddenly felt much larger and much quieter.

Adrienne crossed her arms over her chest and leaned against the counter.

"You realize they can still hear us, right?" she asked. "I've been thinking about options to lose them, and if we go over water-"

"What are you doing here?" Marla asked.

"What do you mean 'what am I doing here'? Saving your ass, apparently!"

"I never asked you to."

Adrienne blinked at her.

"I appreciate that you got me out of the hospital before they called the dog officer. And I appreciate that you got me breakfast and got me out of your apartment. But I didn't ask you to do any of that. I definitely didn't ask you to use your vampire mind-control stuff or start planning some kind of escape! Why don't you just. Back. Off?"

"Excuse me?" White hot anger flared in Adrienne's chest. "Did you miss the part where you almost died?"

"So, what, you bought me a day? Or you bought me a ticket to run for the rest of my life? How is that any better? That woman will hunt me all the way to Mars if she has to!"

"Earth's still a pretty big planet," Adrienne said. "We could-"

"No." Marla stood and stepped into Adrienne's space. "If this is how it goes, then this is how it goes. I sure as shit didn't kill Eddie just so someone else could tell me what to do. Just so someone else could *make* me do what they want."

Wait, what?

"Or didn't you realize that little command of yours hit me too?"

Adrienne's brain stuttered to a stop. She hadn't even considered that. Hell, she hadn't considered anything, just knew they all had to stop. But of course that meant Marla too. She closed her eyes. Was there any of her humanity left? How was she any better than the asshole who'd isolated Marla? Foolish question. She wasn't. She closed her eyes and swallowed hard.

"It was one thing to think I could just start over in a new city. That they wouldn't find me. Obviously, they did, and now that I've seen Carol, I know she's never going to give up. So, if my options are fight her and probably die or run from her for the rest of my life and die, I choose to fight her when I know she's coming. I choose. Not you. Me."

"Fine."

Adrienne opened her eyes, turned, and left the cabin. She just started walking and didn't even acknowledge Darius when he called after her. Her chest was achingly empty and her brain had only room for one thought. Marla was right. Adrienne didn't belong here. She didn't owe Marla shit. She'd already gone above and beyond and proved she really had become a monster. And now she was stuck at this damn campground with no car. It was going to be a long walk home.

Chapter 7

Shortly before dawn, Adrienne's phone finally showed a couple bars of connection. She pulled up a ride share app on her phone. By the time she got in the door, she was ready to face-plant into bed and forget the last twenty-four hours plus had even happened. She couldn't quite make it past the living room, though, without stopping to pick up the picture of Monica and her on their wedding day. It pulled her to it like a magnet.

Five years. It seemed like yesterday. It seemed like forever. She couldn't bring herself to set the photo back down on its shelf and instead brought it into the bedroom and set it on the nightstand by what would have been Monica's side of the bed. She wished she could talk to Monica about any of this. All of it.

She didn't cry. She wasn't entirely sure she even could anymore. But her heart, or what passed for it these days, felt splintered, fragmented even further than it had been. It wasn't fair that someone she'd known less than a week could do that to her. This wasn't like losing Monica. She'd only known Marla a few days.

So it wasn't that, right? Marla had been her patient for a hot minute, and Adrienne got very protective of her patients. The fact that it had gone beyond the hospital walls was what was making it complicated. Marla wasn't just a patient, no matter how Adrienne tried to spin it.

The look Monica was giving her from the photo seemed to say she knew that too. Adrienne closed her eyes tightly and let herself succumb to the sun's demand that she sleep.

It was a beautiful spring day. The sky was clear, the birds were singing, and the cherry trees lining the street were in full bloom when they pulled up to the clinic. Adrienne had insisted on driving because Monica was starting to show. What if they had a fender-bender that was enough to set off the air bags? Better she not be at the steering wheel.

"You really distrust my driving that much, huh?"

"It's not you, babe. It's everybody else on the road."

They'd gone through this dance often enough that it wasn't even an argument so much as a ritual. Once she'd parked, Adrienne followed through the next bit of the ritual by racing around the car to help her wife get out.

"You realize I can get up on my own, right?"

"Give it a few months, and you won't be arguing."

There were people lining the sidewalk in front of the office building. Some were holding gruesome signs. Some were praying. All would have plenty to say about a same-sex couple coming here, so they used the side entrance instead.

The waiting room was full for this time of the morning. One very pregnant person was reading a story to a preschooler. Another was staring angrily at the clock. A couple of adolescents were trying to vanish into their chairs, as if everyone else in the room didn't know that yes, people have sex, and yes, they come to clinics like this for health care to do with sex. It wasn't a huge crowd, but then, this wasn't a very large clinic. Protesters like the ones outside saw to that, keeping the local politicians from giving anything like enough funding.

Maybe they should have gone for a later appointment. They could have, considering Adrienne worked nights and Monica worked freelance. They were both excited for today's ultrasound though and hadn't wanted to wait any longer than they had to. First available time slot of the day it was.

Suddenly, they were seeing their future child on the grainy sonogram screen. Monica looked as awestruck as Adrienne felt. She reached for the screen, then let her hand fall back.

"Do you want to know the sex?"

"No," they answered in unison.

"You want it to be a surprise?" The nurse practitioner gave them a knowing wink.

Then, the wall fell in, taking the ceiling with it.

——◉——

Ambulance ride. Not going to make it. Couldn't leave Monica to deal with this alone.

——◉——

Waking up in the morgue, sharp-featured paramedic waiting for her with a deli container of blood and useless apologies.

——◉——

Walking numbly over to another stretcher in the morgue. Too many stretchers, but she knew which one she needed. Pulling the sheet down to reveal Marla's face where Monica's should have been. Too gray. Too still.

Too late.

——◉——

Adrienne sat up sharply, shaking her head to dispel the dream. She grabbed her phone and checked the time. An hour till sundown. She didn't even know when this fucking fight was scheduled.

A text from Darius answered that.

"If you've gotten over yourself, you have till sunset. You can be here for her, but you can't interfere this time. I'll gag you myself if I have to."

Adrienne didn't bother to question why he'd changed his mind. She threw back the covers and grabbed a fresh t-shirt and jeans.

Maybe she couldn't really do anything. But she could make sure Marla had someone there for her. That might not mean anything to Marla, but it would to Adrienne. She could live with that.

Chapter 8

When Adrienne pulled into the drive for Darius' pack's campground, she was unsurprised to see not only the SUVs from yesterday but several more vehicles as well. Clearly, all of the other pack were here for this fight. So long as they stayed out of it, she supposed that didn't matter.

If they didn't stay out of it, then Adrienne would have no qualms about stepping in again. Except this time she'd dragging Marla out of here.

She followed the sounds of the crowd to a clearing that had been roped off presumably just for this fight. There were two clear sides to the crowd, and for a dizzying moment, she thought of them as home team and visitors at some bizarre version of a football game or boxing match. She supposed that was sort of what it was. There wouldn't be any mouthguards, gloves, or helmets here though.

If she didn't already know so many members of Darius' pack, she wouldn't have been able to tell which side was which. All were in human form, and ranged in appearance from young adult to middle age, though some were likely much older. She made her way over to Ty, who was standing toward the back. She wondered if it felt as weird to him to have to stand back and not interfere. She wasn't sure how long he'd been with the pack and whether he'd been born or bitten. If he was a born werewolf, this pack law bullshit probably seemed normal and would have already been expected before he became a doctor.

There was no such thing as a born vampire, and the only one Adrienne saw much of was the paramedic who'd turned her. They didn't talk much when they did cross paths. Vampires were clearly loners, though Adrienne felt the lack more than the paramedic seemed to. If there were groups or clusters of vampires, Adrienne had no idea who or where they were. As much as she'd become friends with Darius after he'd taken her under his wing, she still wasn't part of his pack. None of this would ever be normal.

There was a buzz of magic she couldn't quite put her finger on. It wasn't quite like the spells on the club, but it felt related somehow. Probably cast by the same witch. But this was absolutely going to be a violent fight, so the parameters had to be different. Maybe something to keep human authorities away?

She heard Darius before she turned to see him.

"Glad you made it," he said. "I think Marla will be too."

Adrienne scoffed but didn't say anything.

"You know what I've gotta do, right?" he asked, holding up what looked like a dishcloth.

At least it was clean.

"Yeah," she said. "Your texts were pretty clear on that. Go ahead."

It was symbolic, really. Unless he'd gotten the thing spelled, she could tear it off if she decided she needed to. She wasn't going to, though. If she had to jump in, it was going to be all brute force, no compulsion. If it was possible to fine-tune it to work on just certain people, she didn't know how. She wouldn't do that to Marla again.

"This will be a fair fight," he said as he tied the cloth in place. "I can't promise how it'll go, but I can promise that it'll be fair."

She made a questioning sound, about all she could manage now through the gag.

"No one can cross the line into the ring but Marla, Carol, Peter, or me."

Adrienne glared at him. He hadn't mentioned that detail in any of his texts.

"One on one," he said. "Peter and I need to be able to go in once the fight is over, but we will not be interfering. Neither will you or anyone else."

A growl caught Adrienne's attention, and she turned to see Marla in her wolf-form walking into the ring. In this light, her fur was more brown than gold, though her eyes still shone bright. There was no sign of how severely she'd been injured before as she slowly paced her side of the ring. She wasn't the one who'd growled, though. That was Carol, the smoke-gray wolf who was being held back by Peter, who had her by the scruff like a puppy..

Marla looked like she wanted to turn and run, or maybe that was just what Adrienne wanted. The golden wolf sat and watched as Carol's alpha convinced her to stay still until the official start of the fight. She scanned the crowd. Adrienne's breath caught when the wolf's eyes met hers, even though they moved on after barely a second.

She might or might not care that Adrienne was here, but she knew. She knew she had someone here rooting for her. That had to count for something.

Darius looked around the space and the buzz of conversation died down.

"We're here today," Darius said from his position at the front of his side of the pack, "to witness the trial-by-contest of Marla Smith for the death of Edward Hill. Edward's mother, Carol here, claims the right of challenge. "

Adrienne wished he'd say something about why Marla had killed him or why they thought this was the way to deal with it. But she knew that was not going to happen.

"When the whistle sounds," Peter said, "the fight shall begin. This is a fight to the death."

Adrienne kept her eyes fixed on Marla as the sound of the whistle pierced her ears.

Carol lunged, and Marla simply sidestepped her. Several in the crowd jeered at that, and Adrienne couldn't help but notice they weren't all on Peter's side.

Another lunge by the gray wolf, who landed again inches from where the golden one had been standing. Now, Adrienne could see what Marla was doing. The booing wolves might see it as cowardice, but this was strategy. Let the enraged wolf tire herself out. The only question was how long she could keep it up. Adrienne wished she could at least shout her support.

Marla's strategy didn't last long. Carol's next move was a shorter jump changing directions to follow Marla's lead sinking her teeth into the golden wolf's shoulder. The angle was perfect for Carol, as Marla couldn't quite turn her neck sharply enough to bite in turn. Instead, she rolled onto her back, seeming to put herself in a worse position. Then, she continued the roll until she somehow had Carol pinned. Marla hadn't worn her out very much though, so in a flash, both wolves were on their feet and facing off again.

Now the crowd noises were more of a mix. Adrienne wished she could add to the ones encouraging Marla, but Darius kept looking over to her. If she took the gag off, she'd be out on her ass in a heartbeat. And after what Marla had said...well. If she won this—and she had better win this—she needed to have no doubt she'd done it on her own. If Marla didn't have full confidence in herself, if she thought she'd been rescued, she'd be furious. It might even damage her ability to fight the next time she had to.

Both wolves lunged, and this time, Marla was the one pinned. Adrienne was being held back by several of Darius' wolves, including Ty, before she even realized she'd tried to reach her.

"Not your fight, vampire," Ty said.

She glared up at him, then snapped her eyes back to the fighting area as the scent of blood reached her. Somehow, in that brief moment, Carol had managed to take a chunk out of one of Marla's forelegs. Marla howled in pain. It took Adrienne a second to be sure, but yeah, she'd gone for the one that Marla had broken just two days ago. Bitch.

Carol snarled and circled. Marla kept the wolf in sight but didn't move. Conserving her energy? Still trying to let the other wolf tire herself out? Could be either or both, but Adrienne approved. Conserving her resources was probably Marla's best chance of surviving.

This time, when Carol lunged, Marla was ready. She splayed her forelegs, making herself shorter, then jumped and got her teeth into Carol's throat. Carol's momentum pulled the two of them into a weird sort of somersault that ended with Marla on top, teeth still firmly locked onto the other wolf's neck. There was no way Carol could break the hold without tearing her own throat out.

Adrienne ached for her to do so. This had to end.

Suddenly, the wolf under Marla shifted back to human form. Blood trickled down her neck as Marla pulled back, releasing her hold.

Adrienne gasped, expecting Carol to shift back as soon as she was free. It was a dirty trick, but it made sense as a way to take advantage of a new wolf.

"Just do it," Carol spat. "You've taken everything else away. Just fucking do it!"

Instead, Marla shifted to human form, too. Both were naked, of course, which gave the scene a surreal appearance. If not for the blood, this would look more like mud wrestling than a fight to the death. Marla rearranged her limbs slightly, so she still had Carol thoroughly pinned. Carol was crying now.

The crowd quieted. Clearly, they had no more idea what to expect than Adrienne did. There were whispers, but Adrienne's entire attention was on Marla. What was her play?

"I don't know if it's your fault Eddie turned out the way he did," Marla finally said. "Maybe. Maybe not. Maybe Eddie's father pulled the same shit on you and he grew up thinking that was normal. Maybe you taught him to think humans were prey. I have no fucking clue."

The whispers grew louder. All Adrienne could think was that Marla must have been up all day thinking about this.

"But you're not the one who hurt me," Marla said. She stood up and remained over Carol, who by now was sobbing. "Maybe it's your fault, but even if it is, you don't deserve to die for it."

"This isn't how it works!" someone shouted. A few others echoed the sentiment.

Darius stepped into the ring, Peter by his side.

Carol was still lying on the ground, glaring at Marla through her tears. Peter went to Carol and clasped her forearm, staying in that position until her breathing evened, though tears were still running through the blood on her face.

"Carol," Peter said as he helped her to her feet, "you still have the right of challenge. What say you?"

That had the ring of some ancient, formal wording. Ritual or ceremony of some kind.

"This is cruelty," Carol said to Marla. "Either let me have my vengeance or kill me. Those are your choices."

"No," Marla said. "Either you taught Eddie to be a shit, with your grief as your punishment, or he learned it some other way. You deserve to heal. From all of it. Those are *your* choices."

The whispers in the crowd picked up, an overall questioning tone to the buzz. Carol could still shift back and attack while Marla was in human form. Adrienne wouldn't put it past her, and she ached to go back Marla up. Ty's grip on Adrienne's shoulder tightened.

"Carol?" Peter asked.

Without a word, the woman turned, walked past her alpha, and left the ring. Peter turned and followed. Ty released his grip on Adrienne, and she ripped her hoodie off and held it up to the edge of the roped-off fighting area, tugging at the gag with her free hand. The boundary spell stung, but she didn't care.

Marla started when she saw her but accepted the garment, seeming to suddenly recognize the chill in the air and that she didn't have fur anymore. She shrank in on herself a little.

"Looks like that's it," Darius said loudly. "Show's over."

"Where are your clothes?" Adrienne asked, mouth finally free.

Marla nodded in the direction of the cabin they'd been in yesterday, climbed over the rope, and started walking. Adrienne kept pace at her side.

Chapter 9

"Here's your jacket."

Adrienne caught it out of the air and looked over at Marla. She was back in the clothes she'd worn yesterday. They were torn almost beyond recognition from yesterday's fight. Adrienne should have thought of bringing more clothes.

"What's your next move?" Adrienne asked rather than dwell on that.

"I don't know." Marla sat down on the green and gold couch. "Darius said I could stay if I won. I'm not sure I want to. Not even sure if that's still open, considering I didn't exactly *win*."

She made no move to invite Adrienne to come in further or to sit, so the vampire stayed just inside the cabin door. In an effort to look less like she was actually blocking the door, she leaned against the frame. She was intruding. No way around that. But she needed Marla to know Adrienne wasn't trapping her.

"If he takes his invitation back because of how that ended, then he's not the Darius I thought I knew." Granted, she'd never really had to see him in his alpha role. He was in charge at the bar, and everyone deferred to him, but what she'd seen these past couple of days was something more. True, she wouldn't have expected him to agree to today's fight, and she wasn't sure if she could forgive him for that. Still, if Marla officially joined his pack, he'd have her back. Marla could use that kind of security.

"I wasn't looking to join a pack in the first place," Marla said. "But maybe...I don't know. I can't live out of a motel forever. I need to either move on or figure out where to live here."

Adrienne hoped she'd stay, but she didn't say anything. Marla didn't need pressure from her. Then, Adrienne did a double take.

"Wait, you're in a motel? That's what that address was that you gave me?"

"What, you thought I'd gotten a permanent address with a pack of werewolves on my ass?" Marla snorted.

No, Adrienne hadn't thought about it at all. It wasn't the kind of thing you asked your unplanned one-night-stand about. All she knew now was she hoped Marla would stay, whether with Darius' pack or in her own place.

"Anyway, he said I don't have to decide right away," Marla said. "I'm not sure what that even means. I should probably find out."

"We can ask him on the way to get your car," Adrienne said. "I mean, if you want. I have my car now, so I can bring you to the hospital for yours."

Marla looked at her curiously, then nodded.

The ride was quiet and awkward. Even if she'd known what to say, Adrienne wouldn't have known the best way to say it. Marla spent the ride looking out the window, probably wishing she was anywhere but here.

When they got to the hospital, Adrienne pulled up next to Marla's car, careful not to box it in. Marla jumped out of the car as soon as it stopped and all but ran to stick the key in the lock. She stopped and then turned to look at Adrienne.

"Thank you," she said, her voice even.

"Of course." Adrienne didn't question whether she meant just the car rid or showing up for the fight or what. She forced a small smile onto her face and drove away without looking back.

***

It had been a week since the fight when the first text had arrived. Marla must have gotten Adrienne's number from Darius. The texts themselves had been ordinary to the point of surrealism. Things like "hi" and "how was your day?" and "do you think it's really going to snow this early in the season?"

Other than that, though, things felt like they'd gone back to what passed for normal. She'd gone to work, done her thing, gone home. That was it. She still hadn't gone back to the bar. Dancing just didn't hold the allure it used to.

She missed the damn werewolf. It was annoying, but she couldn't deny it. Why else would she smile every time one came in, even if she had to wait for a break to actually read it.

So, she replied.

"Hi."

"Rough day at work, how about you?"

"It's New England, it'll snow whenever it wants."

And with each text, the conversations seemed a little more normal, even though there was nothing normal about this.

Three weeks of texting later, Adrienne found herself actually taking her breaks at work, looking forward to whatever ridiculous emoji-sentence Marla had cooked up, then replying with the most bizarre TikToks she could find. Once in a while there was a serious message about figuring out whether to join the pack or finding a job, and she looked forward to those too. She was more careful in responding to them. If Marla asked a question, she'd answer it, but she was careful to keep her responses neutral. Whatever decisions Marla made needed to be her own with no hint of Adrienne having swayed her. If Marla noticed this, she never said anything. Soon enough, they'd be back to emojis and TikToks.

It felt good. It felt normal. It felt human.

Then came the text that made the bottom drop out from her stomach. She was just having her first mug of blood for the evening and scanning the television for something decent to watch on a Tuesday night when her phone chirped.

"Want to meet up at the bar?"

Of course she did. Of course she didn't. Whatever they'd built these last couple of weeks, it still felt fragile. Would it withstand whatever crap would come up face-to-face?

Probably better than it would withstand her saying no.

———◉———

The air was chilly enough that Adrienne thought they just might get that snow Marla had been asking about. Not that she cared much about the cold, but the warmth inside Darius' washed over her, along with the frisson of the wards as she stepped inside. The combination was lovely. Darius saw her come in and gave her a smile and a wave. That was more of a relief than she'd expected.

"Your usual, Elvira?" he asked when she reached the bar and slapped down a bill. "Or do you want the last of the Oktoberfest?"

"Still not funny. Usual's fine."

She scanned the crowd. There were a couple of heads of blond hair, but none that looked to be Marla. She accepted the bottle of beer Darius pressed into her hand without looking and took a swig of it. Then, she heard the voice she'd been missing.

"You should really try the Oktoberfest while it lasts. By next week, it'll be all winter beers."

Adrienne swallowed and turned to see Marla. Her hair was in some sort of complicated half-up braid. Her clothes looked like they were all new, from the dark blue jeans to the green-and-white top and shiny brown leather jacket. Only the pink sneakers looked like the ones she'd been wearing when Adrienne first met her.

"Or you could just stand there doing an impression of a fish. That could work too." Marla quirked a little half-smile at her.

Adrienne snapped her mouth shut, then said, "So, I guess the auto parts job panned out."

Of all the things she could have said, she went with that?

"Yeah, it did." Marla led her over to one of the tall tables that lined the wall on this side of the bar. She took a drink and set her beer down.

Adrienne couldn't think of a single thing to say that wouldn't have been ridiculous. Or pushy. She covered it by taking a drink of her own beer and glancing out the window at the lights over the dark river.

"Cat got your tongue?"

"No." There. That should be safe.

"Good." Marla grinned. "That'd be a damn shame."

Adrienne laughed in spite of herself.

"I'm still not sure about joining the pack permanently," Marla said. "But there's a whole thing where new members basically get a year to see if it's a good fit on both sides. Might as well give it a try."

"Um, yeah. That does sound like a good idea." Surprisingly reasonable, but she decided not to say that part. She'd ask Darius later if this was typical or something he'd done for his pack specifically.

"I mean, if I decide to stay in the area, I'd have to be part of the pack. So, the job will be a factor too. So far, so good, but most jobs seem that way at first, right? At least it's less bullshit than most retail jobs so far."

Adrienne nodded. "Any other factors involved?"

"There could be."

Adrienne could swear she felt her heart actually jump in a way that'd have her reaching for an EKG on anyone who wasn't undead. Or maybe it was just the bass from the song the DJ was mixing. For the first time in a month, she felt like getting up to dance. She set down her beer bottle and held out her hand.

"May I have this dance?"

Marla took her hand and winked. "Long as I leave the ball by midnight."

"That's when things are just getting started!"

Adrienne stepped toward the dance floor but stopped short when Marla tugged her back.

"What?"

"Do you really think once we get dancing that you're going to want to stay here past midnight?" Marla asked. Her tone was less playful than it had been just a minute ago.

"Maybe not," Adrienne said softly. "What about you?"

"I'm not sure yet. Kinda getting used to this whole 'trying things out' business."

"Fair enough. For now, do you want to try out this song?"

Marla's golden eyes sparkled, and she jumped up, pulling Adrienne behind her. Adrienne let herself be led, and something vaguely like relief washed over her, even before they stepped onto the dance floor. As one song blended into the next, she grabbed hold of the melody line and rode it for all it was worth.

Many thanks for reading!

Much of my other work is published with Duck Prints Press, including

Got You Covered

Let the Solstice Come

A Cell of Awareness (in the Aim for the Heart anthology)

You can find these and works by many others at

https://duckprintspress.com/

Also by D.V. Morse

Stand Where You're Afraid

Watch for more at https://dvmorsewriter.com.

About the Author

D. V. Morse (she/her) is a writer of fantasy and science fiction, generally (though not always) with some romance in there somewhere. She's been in various aspects of healthcare for a couple of decades, most recently nursing. A lifelong New Englander who has been writing for as long as she can remember, she loves to explore the liminal spaces in the local landscape and find the stories lurking within. She also loves playing with fiber arts, cycling through knitting, crochet, cross-stitch, and blackwork.

Read more at https://dvmorsewriter.com.